HOW TO HAUNT A HOUSE

Carolyn Crimi

illustrated by
Edward Miller

Happy
Halloween!
Carolyn Crimi

Albert Whitman & Company
Chicago, Illinois

For Chickie—CC

To my great niece Jordyn, with love—EM

Library of Congress Cataloging-in-Publication data
is on file with the publisher.
Text copyright © 2021 by Carolyn Crimi
Illustrations copyright © 2021 by Albert Whitman & Company
Illustrations by Edward Miller
First published in the United States of America
in 2021 by Albert Whitman & Company
ISBN 978-0-8075-3426-7 (hardcover)
ISBN 978-0-8075-3427-4 (ebook)

Printed in China
10 9 8 7 6 5 4 3 2 1 WKT 26 25 24 23 22 21

Design by Valerie Hernández

For more information about Albert Whitman & Company,
visit our website at www.albertwhitman.com.

Ghosties flew from far away
to their class with Madam Grey.
They gathered round from week to week
to learn her special ghost technique.

"Hurry, ghosties, don't be late!
Testing starts at half past eight!
Haunt three houses.
Do your best!
If you succeed, you'll pass the test!

"Here's House One,
so sweet and small.
Ready for your spooky squall.
Make this family shake and shout.
Drive them crazy!
Get them out!

"Now go, my little
ghosties, go!"

WELCOME

Groana slammed the toilet seat.

Moana ate their shredded wheat.

Shrieky spooked their parakeet.

That family screamed
then promptly fainted.
They didn't want to get acquainted.

"Bravo, ghosties! Job well done!
Time to haunt another one!
House Two has big drooling hounds.
Scare them with your spooky sounds.

"Now go, my little
ghosties, go!"

WELCOME

Those huge hounds jumped.
They yowled with dread.

They hid beneath their owner's bed.
"One house to go!" the ghosties cheered.

They stopped and gasped
when it appeared.

"Alas, my ghosties,
this is it.
House Three is tough,
I must admit.

"Be wise, be bold–
you're almost there!
Now go, my ghosties!
Time to scare!"

Groana made
a scary face.

Moana stomped
around the place.

Shrieky rode a pillowcase.

But did that family scream and flee?
Scramble up the nearest tree?
No, not them! They didn't care.
Ghouls like them are hard to scare.

"Ghosties, try a new approach.
Perhaps a slimy toad or roach?
Critters are the perfect touch.
Snakes and bugs and mice and such.

"Now go, my little ghosties, go!"

Groana herded twenty bats.

Moana let loose scrawny rats.

Shrieky brought
in wild black cats.

But what was this?
That family stayed!
They did not yell
or seem afraid!

The woman *fed* those twenty bats.

The small girl *kissed* those scrawny rats.

The wee boy *hugged* those wild black cats.

The ghosties wailed,
"We'll surely fail!"
They turned a paler
shade of pale.

"Ghosties, think!"
cried Madam Grey.
"Do not give up!
You'll find a way!"

The ghosties schemed.

Magic Spells
Witchcraft

BUGS

They messed about.

SLIME

MAGIC
POTION

TRICKS

They turned the
problem inside out.

Something different.

Something new.

And then they knew
just what to do!

They brought in...

Bunnies! Chicks!
Playful pups!

Glitter! Dollies!

Buttercups!

Blankies! Teddies!

Candy canes!

Kittens! Cupcakes!

Daisy chains!

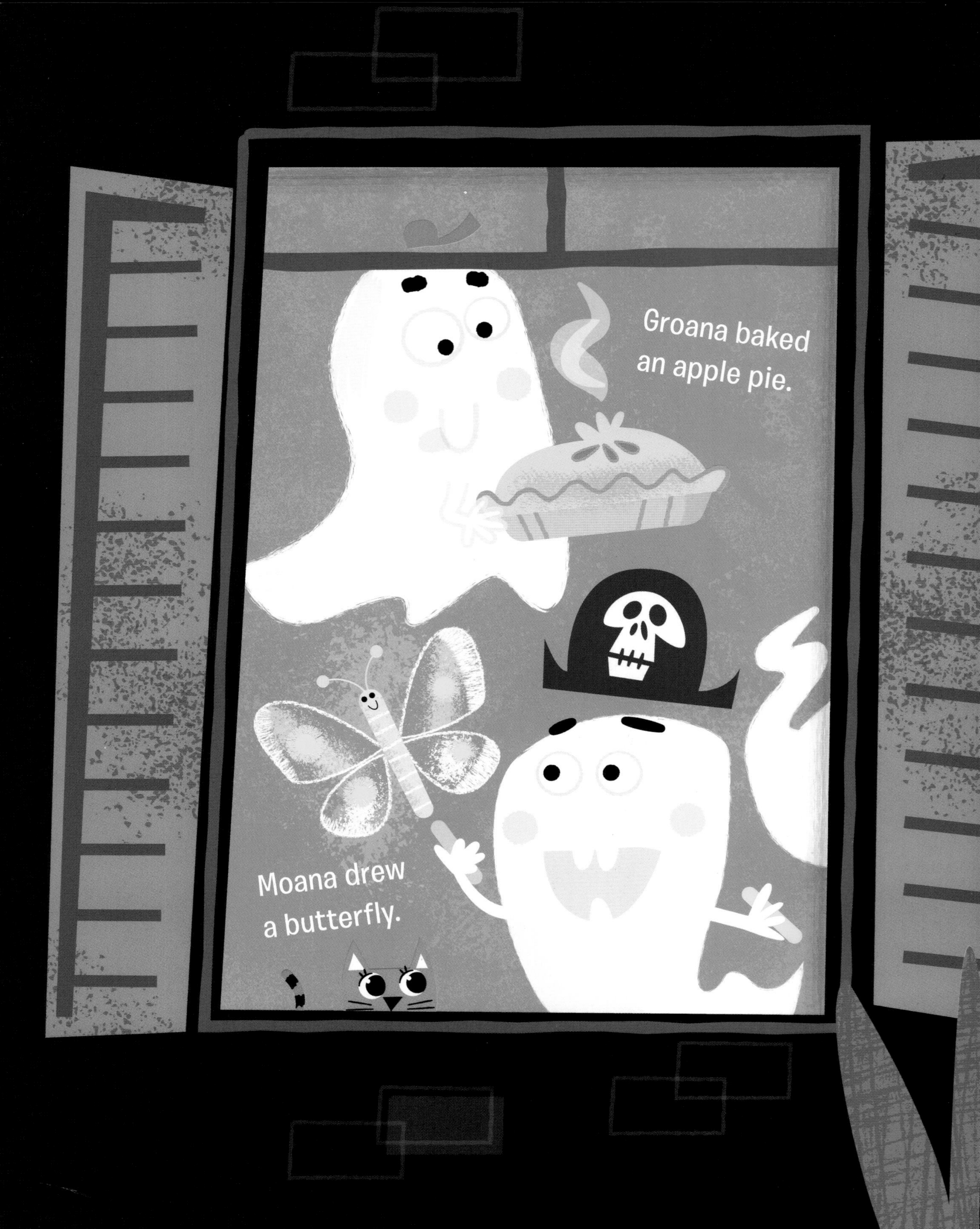

Groana baked an apple pie.

Moana drew a butterfly.

Shrieky sang
a lullaby.

That family freaked!
They shook with fright!
They shrieked and ran into the night!

"You brilliant ghosties passed with style.
Your perfect tricks have made me smile.
They're the best I've ever seen.
You're ready now for Halloween!

Now haunt, my little ghosties,
HAUNT!"